MURDER OF THE SHERIFF

NIKI DUPRE SHORT STORIES BOOK 2

JIM RILEY

THE CRIME SCENE had not been disturbed. Only the forensics techs had been allowed into the jail cell where the body of West Feliciana Parish Sheriff Clem Drake was found earlier. The technicians had not dusted for prints. The cell had hundreds of prisoners run through it since it had last been washed and scrubbed.

Niki Dupre stood at the open cell door staring at the blood still splattered over the iron bars, the two cots, and the floor. Louisiana's most famous private investigator was asked to assist in the probe by Detective Steve Harris, Clem Drake's probable replacement. The strawberry blonde had just wrapped up the murder of Clem's niece.

"What do you see?" Harris asked, looking over her shoulder.

Niki held up a hand in silence and continued to stare at the scene. Then she shifted positions and resumed her vigil. After twelve minutes of silence, she turned to Harris.

CHAPTER TWO

"Two ATTACKERS," she said. "And one guy watched from outside."

"We weren't sure if there were two or three," Harris admitted. "I'm not sure I can take your word for it, though."

"What if I show you how I came to that conclusion?" Niki asked. "If you come to the same conclusion, then we'll agree."

"Sounds good, but I have to warn you. Eighteen years on this job has made me a contrarian. I don't believe anyone until they can prove their side of the argument."

"Fair enough," Niki said. "Let's get the simple stuff out of the way. Let's start with the two guys that killed Clem."

"I'm all eyes and ears," Harris said. "Lead the way."

"Look at the footprints on top of the blood. How many sizes and styles do you see other than Clem's?" Niki asked.

Steve Harris took almost as long as Niki had studying the floor. After a long period of silence, he turned to her.

"I see two of the same style, but different sizes. I also see some that are blurry. They left no prints."

"Those would be from the forensics technicians that

removed Clem's body. Some blood had not completely dried, and they stepped in it with those plastic booties they wear."

"Okay," Harris nodded. "I'm on board so far with you."

"Now the guys on the outside. Look down at your feet, a little to your left. What do you see?" Niki asked. "I see some blood, but not a lot," Harris responded.

"Do you see anything strange about the pattern?"

Harris looked down again. He did not want to be shown up by an amateur detective and struggled for the right clue.

"The only thing I can see is it isn't consistent. There are some spaces with no blood. So, I guess, the blood came from different sprays. Clem's body must have been re-positioned for them to be that close to each other."

"I see another scenario," Niki said. "Do you mind?"

____

CHAPTER THREE

"NOT AT ALL, but remember that I'm cynical. Please don't get upset if I don't agree with your theory," Harris said.

"Not a problem," Niki said without looking at him. "Let's look at the entire splatter outside the cell in segments."

Harris nodded.

"This show is yours to lead."

"All right, let's start with this one," Niki said, pointing to the one on her left. "It is more concentrated closer to the cell and becomes less dense the farther away it got. A familiar pattern, correct?"

Again, Harris nodded.

"There is more blood closer to the source. It dissipates with distance. I think Isaac Newton called it the law of gravity."

"Very good," Niki laughed. "Let's forget the one in the middle for now and look at the one on my right."

Harris shifted his focus. He stared for a while and then switched positions. A frowned cause wrinkles on his forehead.

"I'm sorry. I don't see any significant difference between this one and the other one. I hope you're not basing your theory on those."

"I am," Niki said. "It should be almost the same. It was made at the same time with Clem's body in the same position. That's why they look similar."

Harris had not yet caught up with Niki. He was still staring at the two blood splatters, trying to understand any significance Niki could ascertain from them.

"Okay," Niki said. "Let's look at the middle patterns."

"All right, but I don't see what we can tell from it. There isn't much to it."

"I think there is a lot we can see. But I need your help."

"Whatever, but I'm now more cynical than before," Harris said. Niki moved over and grabbed Harris by shoulders. She led him to the spot outside the cell where the three blood splatters appeared. She placed the detective just inside the two outer streaks. Then she went back inside the cell.

"Move over that way about half an inch," she said, studying his position.

The long-legged private investigator waited for Harris to move. She crouched down with bent knees and looked at his positioning.

"Do you like my pants, or are you staring at my crotch?" Harris said with a forced laugh.

"Neither one interests to me," Niki said without a laugh. "Now, suppose I have a bucket of water, and toss it at your leg. What part of the floor would get wet?"

"Uh—over here," Niki pointed to his left. "And over here, and I guess a little. It'll get wet between—."

The cop's face turned red.

"Dammit, somebody was standing right here," Harris said.

"Exactly," Niki said. "He'll probably wash his pants and

wipe his shoes. But blood is almost impossible to clean off a pair of boots. There are too many places for it to seep."

"So I need to pull the boots off every prisoner we have," Harris said. "We'll get all three of them that way."

Niki shook her head.

"You'll get the two that stabbed Clem, but you want to get the onlooker."

"Why not? You just said it was almost impossible to wipe all the blood from a boot. Why wouldn't I get all three?"

"Because the onlooker wasn't a prisoner. He was one of your corrections officers. Somebody had to have the keys."

CHAPTER FOUR

"Anything else you want to humiliate me more with my own crime scene? I'm regretting ever asking you to take part in this investigation. You're making me look bad."

"As far as I am concerned," Niki said, "we're discovering all this information together. I don't plan to write a report. I think that will be better left to someone in an official capacity."

Harris brightened noticeably. That approach would let him look like a hero instead of a goat. It might also play a key figure in his aspiration to replace Clem as the sheriff.

"I can live with that," he said. "What else did *we* find?"

Niki laughed.

"We found the bigger of the two assailants use a long, thin shiv. The shorter one had a triangular blade, maybe a shard of glass."

"Okay, I'll bite," Harris chuckled. "How did we come up with that conclusion? I might need to include that in the report."

"If we examine the position of the footprints in the blood, the small guy was in front of Clem. The sheriff must have been putting up a good fight. The little guy didn't get in many good licks on him." Niki pointed at the floor as she talked.

"I can buy that," Harris said. "Clem could still defend himself well. How does this mean a short triangular shard? We haven't looked at the autopsy report yet."

"Because of the spray pattern, or more specifically, the lack of one," Niki said.

Harry shook his head.

"I guess that I'm a slow country deputy. I don't see any connection between the two."

"What happens if I use my fingernails to scratch your arm? What kind of spray pattern will I get?"

"None, until I slap the–until I slap you back. Then some of the blood will make an arc depending on which direction I swing my arm to hit you."

"Good," Niki said. "You're more than a country cop. We can agree that the short wounds will give us curved spray patterns if there is a struggle involved."

Harris nodded, then understood. "All the spray patterns in front of Clem have those characteristics. So the little guy attacked Clem from the front, and the big guy slipped behind him."

"Absolutely what I was thinking. You'll see the arterial spray behind were Clem was standing. Hence, the big guy behind the sheriff was using a long, slim shiv of that penetrated Clem's vital organs."

"You know," Harris chuckled. "Together we make an excellent team."

CHAPTER FIVE

"No way. You can't do that," Harris was adamant.

He Niki sat in the sheriff's office. Harris wasted no time claiming it as his own. He knew that perception was often the predecessor of reality, and he wanted the citizens of West Feliciana Parish to perceive him as the next sheriff.

"It's the best approach. Suppose you pull every prisoner's boots. How many of them do you think will have at least a trace of blood on them?" Niki asked.

"Probably every one of them," Harris admitted. "We have a fight in the yard almost every day. Some of them get ugly."

"Exactly," Niki said. "And how long will it take to do a DNA analysis on every pair to match with Clem's blood?"

"Maybe a month or two," Harris guess.

"More like four or five years. You guys still use the East Baton Rouge Parish lab for DNA analysis. The last time I checked on them, they were running at least that far behind."

"And by then, our perps will be standing on a beach in Belize or the Caribbean," Harris nodded. "But I can't let you go into the yard. These guys will eat you alive."

"I can handle myself. You saw that yourself," Niki said.

"That was against the guy and a girl with some rocks in their socks. These guys in here are much better armed."

"I don't have much time to prove to you I can fight," Niki said. "I need for them to attack me."

"You realize that we have over five hundred inmates house here? I don't care how skilled you might be. Five hundred against one is suicidal."

"I don't think all five hundred will come after me. I believe that only the two who killed Clem will have a vested interest. I don't mind two on one. I like those odds."

"But I can't let you take a weapon into the yard. It is against our protocol and common sense."

"I assumed that," Niki said. "I still believe this is the only way we'll get the truth before the special election."

The last statement called Steve's attention. In Louisiana, the death of an office holder meant either an appointment by the governor or a special election, depending on the time between the death and the next scheduled election. In this case, the next scheduled state–wide vote was still eighteen months away.

"So what if they attack you and you somehow survive? What good will that do?" Harris asked.

"That will depend on how long it takes for you to send people to rescue me. I'll need a couple of minutes."

CHAPTER SIX

Four correctional officers escorted Niki to a small alcove in one corner of the recreational yard at the prison. Under an intensely negotiated agreement, Niki and Steve agreed that twenty-five inmates would be released at a time into the yard. All would be instructed to cooperate with her.

The officers carried a small table and two folding chairs. After setting them up, they left the strawberry blonde alone and released the first twenty-five inmates. Niki watched them carefully as they filed out of the building, taking long stares at the attractive female sitting in the corner of their yard. It was a sight none of them had ever seen.

Although curious, none of the over-all clad inmates rushed over to talk to her. They all gawked and whispered among themselves. Niki could only imagine the crude things being said about her in those huddles.

Finally, one gray-haired man hobbled over to the table. He was somewhere between sixty and eighty. Niki always marveled at the effect of prison on the aging process. Some people, especially men, seem to age five years for each one spent behind bars.

"What you doing, little lady?" The old man asked.

"I'm looking into the murder of Sheriff Drake. I thought that one or more of you guys might have some information that will help me. Do you know anything?" Niki asked.

The old man laughed out loud. He kept laughing for a long time and turned to look outside the fence. When he talked, his lips barely moved. From this vantage point, the other inmates could not see him speaking to Niki.

"Little lady, you had better pack up and leave. If you don't, you won't leave this place alive. Do you understand me?"

Niki covered her mouth and appeared to cough. Instead, she whispered to the old geezer, "Thank you for your concern. But I really need to get to the truth."

"The truth is that you are going to get killed. But by then, you'll be begging to die with what these guys will do to you."

"I still have to try," Niki said. "But I thank you."

The old man threw up a hand and walked away.

CHAPTER SEVEN

No ONE else approached from the rest of the first grouping. Nor from the next three groups. Niki noticed that all the guards disappeared from sight, in accordance to the agreement between Harris and herself. The inmates had to have the idea they could get to her.

In the fifth group, one inmate looked at her differently from the rest. He looked at her like an alligator looked at a nutria. Dinner time. Niki could tell the young man would be trouble, and she thought about hitting the panic button provided by Harris. A bevy of guards would arrive within seconds of its activation.

But she let it play out. That was the best way to let other inmates know they could get to her without armed intervention. She let him make his play.

The twenty–something Hispanic wasted no time. He strode up to the table with confidence that his meal was ready.

"Hey, bitch. You want to do it right here or over there behind the shed? I'm good either way."

"The only thing I will do with you is ask you some questions. I'll go slow, so you'll be able to keep up."

The response shocked the Hispanic. He thought the slim, young lady would be a quivering mass by now, begging for mercy. He looked around one more time. Still no guards in sight.

The prisoner turned back to Niki. "The only thing you do will be what I tell you today. If you don't, I'll cut you into little pieces."

He pulled out a homemade shiv. This one had a small iron bar, maybe three inches long, taped to a piece of wood. The point of the apparatus was filed to a sharp end. It was a formidable weapon.

"You're about to embarrass yourself in front of your friends. They'll laugh at you when a girl kicks your butt," Niki said.

The youngster appeared less confident. Instead of moving forward, he edged sideways, his feet unable to stay still. But when he glanced over his shoulder, all his fellow inmates were staring at him. He was already past the point of no return. To back down now would bring only humiliation.

He sprang forward, the shiv in his right hand. His target was her left shoulder. The prisoner did not want to kill her until he finished with his other business with the private investigator. The only problem with his plan was that her shoulder was no longer at his aim point. Nor was her body.

Niki shot to her right, then tripped the charging man. He went down on the hard surface, skinning the right side of his face. However, he held onto the shiv and quickly rose to his feet, brandishing it like a baton.

"I told you it would get embarrassing," Niki said. "Look, all your friends are already laughing at you."

The kid made a fatal mistake. He changed his focus from Niki to the other twenty-four inmates. He never saw the foot before it smashed into his lower mandible. He might not have felt it either. He went down and out so quickly that Niki did not know if he would remember the blow.

There was a different look from the rest of the inmates. Three of them walked over and picked their friend up. Two grabbed the inmate's legs, and the other carried his arms. They took him inside, still without a corrections officer in sight.

Niki wished the incident had not happened. But there was little time to dwell on it. The next twenty-five men were ushered into the yard before the guards once again disappeared. Only Niki and the men occupied the small outdoor space.

CHAPTER EIGHT

In less than two minutes, two broke out from the rest. They stalked toward Niki, exchanging nervous glances with each other and then all around in search of law enforcement. Finding none, they became more sure of themselves as they approached.

"What you doing here, bitch?" The bigger of the two men asked.

"I came to talk to you too," Niki said. "If I'm not mistaken, you have a long, slim instrument and your smaller partner has a short flat one. Am I correct?"

Her knowledge stunned the big inmate. All the cameras were supposed to be off. All the guards were busy in another part of the facility. No one has seen them. How did this woman possess this intimate knowledge? Had his partner ratted them out to someone? The big man would take care of him later. First, he had to deal with this woman.

"How you know all that, bitch?" He asked.

Niki laughed easily.

"You guys might as well have taken photos and posted them

on the message board. But then, I guess the time in here has lowered your already low IQ's."

"Are you dissing us? That ain't no good for your health."

"Neither is stupidity, but you seem to possess an abundance of it. Is this where you threaten me with those bad blades of yours and try to scare me?" She asked.

"You'll be scared, bitch," the big man said. Then he faked a lunge at her.

Niki ignored the deke. She had already seen an example of their handiwork. She was sure the small guy would keep her busy in front while the bigger fellow slipped behind her back. She did not plan to accommodate their goals.

Instead of jumping back, the long-legged detective rolled toward the smaller one. Her foot smashed into his stomach just below the sternum. His hand was barely from behind his back, but not near close enough to deflect the blow. He dropped the shiv, fell backward, and gasped for breath. It was slow in coming.

Niki sprang to her feet and spun to face the bigger man.

"What's wrong?" She smirked. "Are you afraid to take me on without your little buddy? Afraid a girl will hurt you?"

"You can use that fancy kicking on him, but I'm ready for you. Ain't no way you're going to kick me like that," he said.

For an answer, Niki delivered a straight kick to his throat. If he had held the blade with a long edge, she would not have tried that move. When his right hand instinctively closed to protect his neck, the only part of the bar that hit her leg was the ground surface. The sharp point came nowhere close to any part of her body.

Now she had a choice to make; which of the men to keep alert to question. The little guy would probably give in the easiest, but he was clearly a follower. He might not know enough answers to satisfy her curiosity.

The big guy would be harder to break, but he was much more likely to have the answers she sought. Then she remembered what Butch Cassidy said when they asked him why he robbed banks. He replied, *"Because that's where the money is."*

In this case, the answers were with the big guy. It mattered little that it would be more difficult to obtain. She spun and landed her right foot in the small guy's temple.

CHAPTER NINE

Niki turned to face several of the inmates who came to retrieve the pair.

"Take that one," she said. "But leave the big guy."

The four prisoners who picked up the little man watched Niki like they would a water moccasin. They had seen her strike and did not want to be on the receiving end of her kicks. Whispering among themselves and pointing, they moved the unconscious man toward the cell block. Three guards came out of the building. Two herded the prisoners inside. The third man walked toward Niki.

She held up a hand.

"This fight isn't finished yet. He just threatened me again, and I need to deal with it."

The guard looked at the big fellow. He saw that the big prisoner could barely breathe, much less utter a threat. Then he remembered his orders, shrugged, and turned back around.

Niki leaned over to the big guy and realized her mistake. If the big man could not talk, she could never get answers from him. She started with simple *yes/no* questions. A nod or a shake of the head would be all that was required.

"Will you live?" She began with an easy question.

The big man nodded, though he did not look certain.

"Was that you and your little partner who killed Sheriff Clem in the cell last night?" She asked, not expecting an answer.

When her expectation of silence was met, the detective reached out and grabbed the man's pinky finger. By the time she finished, the digit was bent straight back on his hand, and he was crying like a pampered two-year-old brat.

"You—you—you can't do that," he rasped.

"Sure, I can," Niki said cheerfully. "I told the guard you and I are in the midst of battle. Is it my fault that your side is not armed and you refused to agree to the articles of surrender?"

The prisoner looked at her with a blank there.

"What that means on a second grade level–hold on, did you get past the second grade? Am I wasting my time?"

The big fella held up five fingers. She took it to mean he made it at least until the seventh grade before he maxed out on his limited potential.

"Good," she said. "What that means is that if you don't answer my questions, all ten of your fingers will end up pointing in the wrong direction. You saw how much that one hurt. Do you really want to go through that nine more times?"

The prisoner looked down at his broken finger and whimpered. Then, with tears in his eyes, he nodded at the strawberry blonde.

CHAPTER TEN

"Floyd Baxter," Niki said ten minutes later. She sat in the Sheriff's office with detective Steve Harris.

"Floyd Baxter?" Steve repeated, shaking his head. "He's been here longer than I have. He's old school. Are you sure that's the name that José gave to you? You could be mistaken."

"My hearing is still good," Niki laughed. "What can you tell me about Floyd Baxter? What kind of guy is he?"

"He's a solid as they come. Floyd breaks a few rules now and then, like taking a sip on the job, but overall he's one of the best deputies in the parish."

"Could Floyd have been bribed?" Niki asked.

"I never thought so before now," he said. "If you are right, however, somebody got to him one way or the other."

"Does he have a family? Wife, kids, anything?" Niki asked.

"It's just Floyd and his wife, Mary. All his kids are grown and gone. Been gone for a while, I believe."

"Where do they live? Is it close to the department?"

"No, they have a little place off Arnold Road. It'll take us twenty or thirty minutes minimum to get there."

"Then we had better hurry," Niki said. "I've got a feeling that if we're too slow, the word will get out that José talked. Floyd's life won't be worth a plug nickel. Neither will his wife's."

"Hold on," he said. "I've got to call the mayor and tell him what we're doing. I mean, accusing a deputy of being involved in Sheriff Clem's murder is no small thing."

"Do what you have to do. Just do it fast," Niki said.

"Wait for me," Harris said. "I'll be out in less than five minutes."

─────────

CHAPTER ELEVEN

MORE THAN THIRTY MINUTES LATER, Steve Harris emerged from the building, walking at a fast pace.

"Sorry," he said, getting into the sedan. "The mayor wanted to get the city attorney online. The lawyer hemmed and hawed, gave us both sides of the answer, and then said that he would have to look at precedent law. In the end, he gave us just what I figured, enough rope to hang ourselves."

"Lawyers are pros at that," Niki nodded. "Now he can tell you that you went against his advice no matter what you do."

"Except that it took him a half-hour to do it. We could have already been to Floyd's by now. I hate to say it, Niki, but you've got me a tad nervous about all this."

"That means you're a sharp cop," Niki said. "I believe those guys are tied to the MS–13 gang. They don't play by the rules the rest of us have to follow."

"Speaking of which," Harris coughed. "How am I supposed to explain how one of my inmates got his little finger bent hundred and eighty degrees from where it should be?"

"Easy," Niki said. "He attacked a visitor to the jail. In the process of subduing him, José's finger was bent a little. I don't see what's so hard to explain about that scenario."

"And if he says that you broke it after the fact?" Harris asked.

"C'mon, Detective. Do you really think a tough guy, probably in cahoots with MS-13, will ever admit a girl did that to him? I bet he's already told the rest of the guys twelve guards ganged up on him."

Harris thought about her words and eventually nodded. They spent the rest of the ride in relative silence.

CHAPTER TWELVE

Floyd's place was part of a larger estate that subdivided many years earlier. Each of the plots was five acres at a minimum, with an average over twenty. The deputy's lot fell in a tad above the average, twenty-two beautiful acres.

Niki saw a two-acre pond behind the ranch-style house situated close to a red barn with a green roof. Floyd had chosen well. His home sat among rows and rows of pecan trees. With the price of the delicious nut at nearly twenty dollars a pound, the deputy sat on a fortune. All the trees were at least forty years old, though Niki was no fauna expert. But she knew they were all tall and wide.

A barbed wire fence surrounded the entire plot. Niki saw two buckskin horses and several Santa Gertrudes cattle. Those red cows and bulls were expensive, but cost little more than any other breed to maintain. Another fortune on the ground for the long-term deputy.

"Nice place," Harris said, pulling into the front yard. "I'm not sure how he can afford all this on his salary."

"I can," Niki said. "He probably bought land cheap when

the estate split up. He then used the money he earned from the pecans to start the cattle herd. After that, all he needed was a little patience. And change out his herd bull every three or four years. The rest is easy."

"And just how does a city girl like you know anything about Santa Gertrudes cattle and herd bulls?"

"You forget that my fiancé is Dalton Bridgestone, the United States Senator. He owns the biggest exotic game ranch in Louisiana."

"What does that have anything to do with herd bulls?"

"I'm making an assumption. In his deer and elk herds, he has to bring in different studs. He doesn't want to get into straight-line genetics between a sire and a daughter. That might mess up the entire gene pool of the herd," Niki answered.

"I guess you could use West Baton Rouge Parish for proof of the consequences of interbreeding with kin. I think some of those people have trouble finding their way out of bed."

"Animal breeders have the same trouble, though they are trying to engineer bigger and better bodies and horns, rather than intelligence."

"Sounds like Hitler," Harris laughed. "That didn't work out so well."

Niki sat upright and tensed.

"Something is seriously wrong."

"What makes you say that?" Harris asked. "More intuition?"

"We haven't heard a dog bark, and we've been sitting here for over three minutes. That's not right."

"Maybe Floyd is allergic to dogs. Unlike you city dwellers, all of us in the country don't own dogs."

"Then why are there two empty kennels with full bowls of dog food and water?" Niki asked, drawing her S&W thirty-eight revolver.

CHAPTER THIRTEEN

HARRIS FOLLOWED NIKI'S EXAMPLE, pulling his Glock 17 from the holster at his waist. They alternated their advance to the front door, taking cover behind every tree and the two cars parked between them and the house.

Niki held up a hand halfway there. She held two fingers, then put her hand flat and pointed to the side of the house. Harris ran to her side.

"Is it Floyd and Mary?"

Niki shook her long mane.

"Two red-bone hounds. Some of the best coon dogs on the planet."

Harris craned to see over her shoulder and peered at the point where she pointed. Two beautiful red-tick puppies lay on the ground, their throats cut in wide slashes.

"Somebody wasn't playing around," Harris knelt back down.

"And not that long ago. The blood is still wet. We must have just missed them," Niki said.

"If we missed them," Harris countered. "For all we know, they might still be inside the house this very minute."

"And how did they get here?" Niki asked, holstering the thirty-eight caliber.

"Uh—" Harris looked back at the two vehicles in the front yard. The red Ford pickup was the same one that Floyd drove to work every day. The silver Honda Accord belonged to Mary, who drove it when she came to see Floyd at the Sheriff's office. There were no other vehicles anywhere near other than his own sedan. The killers were gone.

But Harris did not put his pistol special away. He ascended the step, careful to stay to one side. When the West Feliciana Parish cop reached the front door, he stepped to one side, stretched his arm and knocked on the frame.

Niki walked right past him through the door. "Dead people aren't going to hear you out here knocking,"

"Hey, you can't—" Harris yelled as she passed him. Then he followed her inside. He bumped into her back.

"Do you smell what I'm smelling?" Niki asked.

"Yes," Harris said. "There is no other smell like blood."

They follow their noses, Harris with the service pistol drawn. The sharp odor led them to the first bedroom down the hallway. Harris raised a fist to knock.

Niki pushed past him. "They won't hear you."

She stopped only a foot into the master bedroom. The scene was one of the most macabre that she had ever witnessed. To add to the visual was a horrible stench.

Floyd Baxter sat on the floor at the foot of the bed. At least what was left of him. His entrails splayed in front of his body. One of his attackers had slashed open his belly while the old cop was still alive and had reached inside. Not once, but several times. Floyd's stomach was now an empty space.

His pants were pulled down to his knees. His private parts were been sliced off and stuck inside Floyd's mouth.

Mary Baxter's body was spreadeagled on the bed over Floyd's head. She had slits and cuts over her entire body surface. Two of those had removed her breasts. At first glance, Niki could not tell where they went.

CHAPTER FOURTEEN

"My God," Harris exclaimed. "What kind of animal would do something like this? I can't believe anyone could."

"It wasn't an animal," Niki said. "It was three of them."

Harris closed his eyes and shook his head. "I hate to ask, but how do you already know that?"

"Three different footprints, all three on the small side. I'm guessing three teenage boys," Niki said.

"Do you believe girls are too nice to do this?" Harris asked.

"Not at all," Niki replied. "I have seen some evil females during my time as a private investigator. Some of them could easily have tortured just as much as this, but not in the same way."

"How would it be different?" Harris asked.

"For one, they would not have repeatedly raped Mary. That's a physical limitation. Second, they might have sliced Floyd, but they wouldn't have eviscerated him."

"And where do we get that gem of information?"

"History," Niki replied. "From Vind the Impaler, to Jack the Ripper, to the present day, all the culprits were male."

"I wasn't very good at history in school," Harris admitted. "I mean, who cares what happened five hundred years ago?"

"Do you know who Harry Truman was?" Niki asked.

"I'm not that uninformed. He was President when we dropped two nukes over Japan."

Niki smiled for the first time since entering the room.

"Very good. He did it to prevent millions of deaths because history taught him that a frontal assault would cause just that."

Steve nodded. "I can see that. Smart man, huh?"

"There is nothing new in this world except for the history we don't know. That's why I know this was three teenage boys who did this."

"I get that it was guys. Why do you stick to the assumption they were teenagers? They could have just been small."

"Look at the empty candy bags, wrappers, and chips. Looks like a teenage smorgasbord. Most grown-ups would want something more substantial over a two-day period."

"Well. How do you know they were here two days? It looks like to me, Floyd and Mary were killed right before we got here. We were only minutes late."

"You're right about their deaths, but they have been torturing Mary for at least two days. Look at the abrasions on her wrists. All that damage wasn't done today."

CHAPTER FIFTEEN

"Do you ever read the coroner's report?" Harris asked after they went outside, relinquishing the crime scene to the able members of the forensics team. He continued, "I mean, what could it tell you that you don't already know?"

"Lots of stuff. You know, like the third knife," Niki said.

"What third knife? How do you know there was more than one?"

"Because I saw two different cut patterns on the bodies. They used the same two to slice and stab both Floyd and Mary. But I didn't see a third one."

"Maybe the third person was a girl. Remember, you're the one that said that females wouldn't do this kind of thing."

"It wasn't a girl," Niki said. "There were three boys there, and I'm guessing they were Latino or something close."

"Okay, I'll bite. Why were they Latino or something close?"

"Because all the packages of salsa. They put the stuff on everything. No barbecue sauce, no steak sauce, no ketchup or mayo. Only salsa. Generally, that would mean Latino boys."

Harris sighed.

"You've made your point. I give up. Can we agree that these kids were members of MS–13?"

33

CHAPTER SIXTEEN

"How come we never hear anything about this MS-13 gang?" Donna Cross asked when Niki returned to the townhome that she also used as an office. Donna, an hourglass blonde, was a critical partner to Niki, providing all available data from anywhere on the Internet. She could successfully hack into any system in the world without leaving a trace.

"They don't like the spotlight," Niki replied. "They would rather only certain people know of their activities. People like their victims, and any future targets or potential witnesses."

"So, people are scared to go up against them?" Donna asked. "What about the police? Why don't they do something?"

"Different reasons," Niki replied. "Some of them are scared of what the gang will do to them or their families. Some have been bought. Taking money is easier than dying."

"But there have to be a few honest, brave cops. I mean, look at Samson," Donna said, referring to the behemoth chief of homicide for the East Baton Rouge Parish Sheriff's Department and Niki's mentor and friend. "He is just as brave and honest as any man I've ever met. Nobody can scare him or buy him."

"Even Samson needs evidence and witnesses. He can't haul down an entire organization based on assumptions."

"How are kids attracted to the group like that?" Donna asked. "I did some stupid stuff as a teenager, but nothing like joining a bunch of thugs just to kill and maim people."

"But you had the advantage of a solid family. Most of these kids know only the street. If a gang can make them feel wanted, then they are drawn into its sticky web. Once they are a part of it, there is only one way to leave."

"Not exactly like dropping out of the sorority?"

"Not even close. Their bodies leave, but they don't."

Donna's hands flew over the laptop computer. After only a few minutes, she looked up at Niki.

"There is a lot of innuendo and few facts about the local MS-13 group. I can give you the history of the overall organization on a national perspective, but not much about them in Baton Rouge."

"And I would bet it would be the same for New Orleans, Lafayette, Alexandria, Monroe, or Shreveport. These guys keep a low media profile at the local levels."

"You're probably right. I haven't checked yet. I ran across one name that popped up several times, but it was almost always as an afterthought. It's like he's there, but he's not there. Does that make any sense at all?"

"Sure. He would want his enemies to know they had better not mess with him. They may tangle with the gang members, but they dare not mess with the head honcho. As President Trump said, some of them are *bad hombres*."

"That description seems to fit this guy. His name is Juan Valdez. I don't have a clue how to find him."

"Which means I don't either," Niki said. "I've got to figure out a way to smoke him out."

"Are you sure you want to do that?" Donna asked. "I can't

repeat all the dead presidents, but I remember someone said *where there is smoke, there is fire.* From what I've read about this guy, his fire is fatal."

"But if I don't do anything, then I'm no better than all those scared cops, and Valdez will win again."

CHAPTER SEVENTEEN

Juan Valdez was comfortable. Well, as comfortable as any gang leader could ever be. There was always one guy or a small group within the ranks contemplating overthrowing the current leadership and taking over.

As the kingpin, Juan had all the privileges of power. He got all the young girls first, while they were still fresh and challenging. He was in charge of the growing profits. Prostitution, drugs, and the protection racket were just as profitable as ever. He was one of the first among his contemporaries in other cities to delve into identification theft.

But he soon learned just how lucrative that end of the business could be. And it carried little physical risk to boot. All it took was a list from the dark web, a series of computers tied to the net through Wi-Fi, and some minimally capable operators.

As it turned out, the girls were better than the guys. The males would get frustrated with the art of inputting believable data without hitting the wrong keys. Being a volatile bunch, they often tossed the keyboards across the room. But the girls were more patient. Besides that, the ugly ones were the best.

Instead of making him five or ten dollars a pop on the street, they now brought in millions.

For a while, Valdez considered getting out of the other businesses altogether. But if he did that, the group would lose the fear factor they had so arduously built over the years. Without that, Juan knew that he would be vulnerable to a takeover.

Hence, things rolled right along. The only snag was the situation up in St. Francisville. Two of his guys were not able to get rid of a girl. Then he had to take a risk and murder a deputy and his wife, a move that made him vulnerable under most circumstances.

This, however, was not usual circumstances. Like many other cop shops, Valdez had a man on the inside. His insider assured him that all could be swept under the rug and the MS-13 name would never be mentioned as a part of it. That made him more comfortable. Until he was surprised when a fat, ugly girl printed out a paper and brought it to him.

"Who is this bitch?" The leader of the gang demanded. He sat down with his inner circle, those closest to him and in whom he could trust. Actually, he was not sitting. The leader fiercely paced back and forth. He had made several copies of the report and gave each of the guys one. None of them wanted to answer him.

The report was an interview with a local reporter with the Baton Rouge Advocate. It was the only daily newspaper in the state capitol. In the interview, Niki Dupre talked about the death of Clem Drake, the Sheriff of West Feliciana Parish, and the subsequent investigation.

CHAPTER EIGHTEEN

"Are you positive that MS-13, the violent gang from south of the border, was involved in the murder?" The reporter asked Niki.

"Absolutely," Niki answered. "Only the gang is no longer south of the border. They are right here in Baton Rouge. In every large city in Louisiana."

"Why are you so sure they were behind this death?" The reporter asked.

"I had the opportunity to interview a couple of the men who carried out the plot. They willingly gave me a lot of information about the murder and the reasons behind it."

"That doesn't sound like the typical gangsters that we read about. Most of them would rather die than blab."

"The murder of someone in law enforcement is a death penalty crime in Louisiana. They were pretty well doomed either way. I guess they wanted to put off their execution as long as possible. Besides that, I don't think these guys are as scared of the local gang leader as they might be."

"Amazing. Did the two offer any names?" The reporter asked.

"The first was that of a good, honest cop named Floyd Baxter. He and his wife, Mary, were tortured and executed because they knew that the gang was responsible for the murder. So they added two more deaths to protect the coward that runs the group."

"Did they tell you the name of the coward?"

"The yellow skunk goes by the name of Juan Valdez," Niki answered. "But he won't come after me. He'll send some of his thugs. He is way too much of a coward to come after me himself."

CHAPTER NINETEEN

"WHAT'S wrong with you guys? I asked you who this bitch is and I don't get a single answer. Have you all turned it to a bunch of sweet pussycats instead of real men?"

"She's a private investigator," the man second to Juan said. "She's some kind of street martial arts expert. That's how she got to José and Rafael."

"I want those two dead before the sun comes up," Valdez growled. "I don't care how you do it. Just make sure they're dead."

"It won't be that easy," the same man said. "There are a lot of outsiders out there talking to them. People we don't control, and who have been after us for a while."

"All the more reason to kill them tonight. If they aren't dead by morning, some of you will be," Valdez stormed.

"I'll take care of it, but it'll be expensive. Favors like these don't come cheap," the man said.

"I don't care," Valdez screamed. "They gave my name to that whore. Nobody can do that and live. They have to die."

"Consider it done," the man sighed. "What do you want to

do about the investigator? We're not the only ones who will read this report. When our members do, they'll have some questions."

"Do you really believe they'll think I'm a coward?"

"If you don't respond, what else can they think?" the man asked.

"I'm not scared of her or anyone else. Bring her to me and I'll show her why she should never have mentioned my name."

"Wouldn't it be better if you brought her in yourself?" the man asked. "Then there'll be no question about your courage."

"Because I'm needed to run this organization. Without me, it will fall apart in days. None of you are capable."

"Do you want Niki Dupre brought in alive or dead?"

"Alive," Valdez stated confidently. "She must be alive. I want to be the one that slits her pretty little throat."

CHAPTER TWENTY

"Are you completely nuts?" Harris yelled over the cell. "Have you lost that brilliant mind of yours?"

"I had to do it. No one knows where to find Juan Valdez. If I couldn't go to him, I had to get him to come to me. You know, *the mountain and Mohamed* sort of thing."

"Well, the mountain is about to crush your pretty little butt."

"Then at least I'll know where he is," Niki replied. "I'll know a lot more than I do right now, which is nothing."

"He won't come. He'll send his minions. A lot of them. And from what I understand, being a female will not work in your favor."

"Then they'll underestimate me. I don't expect Valdez to come in person the first time. Eventually, he'll have to."

"If the guys he sends are successful?" Harris asked. "Then he will have you brought to him. We'll be lucky to recover little bitty parts of your body."

"Then you'll know who did it, and then you can arrest him," Niki smiled into the cell. "Something good will come out of it."

<h1 style="text-align:center">CHAPTER TWENTY-ONE</h1>

"You NEED to stay at your place for a while," Niki said to Donna. They were at the townhome trying to prepare for an outright assault on the detective.

"I can do more good if I'm here to help," the hourglass blonde replied. "You may need all the help you can get."

"I need your help," Niki replied. "But facing men with guns, knives, and machetes is not your forte. That part of our business is mine. And I'm not going to pass it off to you."

"How can I help you then?" Donna asked.

"Do what you do best. Get online and find out everything you can about the local MS-13 gang," Niki said.

"I've already looked. There is a big lot of nothing."

"Then try harder," Niki urged. "I need to know how many guys Valdez has. If you can get names, that would be great."

"What I'm not sure of is where to begin," Donna stated.

"How about starting with something you know? According to Detective Harris, the local group has branched into identity thefts. Then they get on the names of the victims. They do all of that over the Internet."

"I can do that," Donna broke into a huge grin. "They have to buy the list on the dark web. I can track him down."

"Isn't the dark web almost as big as a regular one?"

"Yeah, but if they're just getting started, they haven't yet perfected how to hide the trail. I'll be able to find it easily."

"There is one more way you can help," Niki said.

"Anything you want, as long as I can eat while doing it."

"Rent a cargo van. One without windows, preferably with a cage separating the driver from the rear."

CHAPTER TWENTY-TWO

Niki left the townhome a little after dark. The half moon and the stars were hidden by massive clouds. She glanced around the lit parking lot and noticed the Chevy parked in the corner. Three men sat inside and stared at her every step. None of them made any attempt to hide their interest in the long-legged detective.

She gave the one glance and then ignored them. These were not Valdez's elite force. He had sent new recruits because he thought the job would be easy. After all, she was only one slim woman against three husky Latinos.

As soon as the light on her Ford Explorer came on, the ones on the old Chevy beamed through the darkness. So much for stealth. Niki smiled as she exited the parking lot. The Chevy pulled out only feet behind her. If there had been any doubt of the men's intention, it was no longer there.

Niki drove east until she reached Joor Road. At the intersection, she turned left and sped up. She needed to time it just right. Sure enough, the Chevy turned right behind her, only feet from her bumper.

After they passed Greenwell Springs Road, she knew the only light on the entire stretch was three hundred feet ahead. She waited until the last second and then blew past the pickup truck that was moseying down the road.

Then she slowed to the same speed as the truck, not allowing enough space for the Chevy to fit between the two vehicles. The Latinos had to lag in third place, trying to figure out what the strawberry blonde was attempting.

They soon found out. As the trio of automobiles neared the light, it turned from green to yellow. Niki slowed as if she was about to stop, then revved the powerful engine of the Ford Explorer. The white SUV shot through the intersection, leaving the truck and the old Chevy stuck behind the red light. She smiled, imagining the language being used by the three guys in the car.

However, she did not speed away. Slowly, she drove until only her tail lights were visible before a sharp curve. As soon as the light turned green again, she took off and turned on the next left. She was already more than a half mile away before the Latinos spotted her lights and whipped left to follow her.

Then she was around the next curve. This was the tricky part. She needed enough distance between her and the pursuers, but not too much. She did not want them to catch her. Nor did she want them to lose her in the chase.

The investigator turned right on State Road, which Niki knew was a dead end. She could only hope the dead end was meant for the men and not for her.

CHAPTER TWENTY-THREE

Small houses lined both sides of the road. Most of the lights were still on this early in the evening. Niki smelled a barbecue grill and thought about how good a T-Bone steak would taste. But she had business to do first.

The road ended at a long pipe stretched across its span. It was supported by a post with hinges on one hand and chained on the other to a separate iron beam. Behind the posts was the maze.

The maze was an abandoned development comprised of sixty-two acres. The original plan was to build almost two hundred houses on the acreage. The developers filed the paper-work and began construction. They put in paved roads, under-ground electrical, and sewage and built a water plant.

Then the bad news came. The approval process for the project was denied. The owners of the houses that lined the road complained that the project would create too much traffic on the two-lane road and would have a detrimental impact on their property values.

The developer went bankrupt. That left an unguarded

playground for teenage lovers, people needing a place to congregate without being observed or folks who needed a convenient place to dump their trash. The maze was it.

After several complaints of loud noises all hours of the night from the closest neighbors, the owner put up the gate. That did not stop the four wheelers, but it put an end to the other vehicular traffic in the maze. Anyone wanting to see the sights now had to walk. That's exactly what Niki did.

CHAPTER TWENTY-FOUR

THE LEAN INVESTIGATOR exited the Explorer, jammed the keys in her pocket, and jumped the bar. She saw the old Chevy closing in on her SUV and knew that she would be illuminated by its lights. The detective jumped the ditch and squeezed into the dense canopy between two small oaks.

The three Latinos pulled in behind the SUV. All three got out and argued. One wanted to call Valdez for instructions. The second wanted to go back to the townhome parking lot and wait for Niki to return.

The third castigated his partners for their cowardice. He called them every name he could think of and a few he made up on his own. There was no way that he would report a failure to the crime boss. To do so would mean the end of his reputation, if not more dire consequences.

They spoke in Spanish, though Niki could only hear one or two words every so often. Two of those she heard were *no muerte*. She smiled when she realized they were sent to bring her back alive. That fact pushed the odds way over to her advantage.

Finally, the assertive Latino convinced the other two the pursuit and capture of the strawberry blonde was the only acceptable solution. Any other outcome would have to be explained, and none of them yet had enough credibility to pull it off.

One of them, the presumed leader, flicked on his flashlight, much to Niki's chagrin. Not that she was scared of being spotted, but all three men were likely to stay huddled by the light instead of spreading out during the search. She much preferred to take them one–on–one.

Even though she felt confident that she could whip all three together, to do so would take valuable time. These three were not experienced fighters. One of them might fire his weapon in his anxiety, and that was the last thing the detective wanted. A random shot might be fatal to her or one of the other two Latinos. Neither scenario fit into her plan.

Niki waited until the three, walking on the paved road, came even with her. Then she exploded out of her hiding place, and burst onto the road. Her first kick caught the nearest Latino high in his thigh. He yelped and fell onto the pavement.

Her second kick caught a turning Latino in his crotch. He bent over, and she trapped him with a knee to his forehead. The blow was not enough to send him to Lala land but to addle the henchman for a while.

Then she struck out at the leader. He was already facing her, with the flashlight in one hand and the Ruger in the other aimed at her head. She noticed the pistol was equipped with a suppressor and said a silent thanks to the One above. The last thing she needed right now with a bunch of cops responding to a gunshot.

The leader yelled something in Spanish. It might as well have been in ancient Greek to Niki. She was not listening. Instead, the detective tucked into a ball and rolled directly at the gunman. When within reach, her legs sprang, propelling her foot into the Latino's wrist.

The weapon spat one bullet before flying into the darkness. Niki heard a splash into a canal that served as the drainage for the property. By then, her other foot smashed into the arm attached to the flashlight. It followed a similar path as that of the pistol. The splash told the story.

After that, Niki disappeared as quickly as she had come. Two of the three hoodlums were still armed, and she did not want to catch a bullet in the back. That was not part of the plan.

CHAPTER TWENTY-FIVE

The detective did not go far. She lowered behind a blown-down red oak and waited. The wait did not last long. She had time to text Donna and get her started that way with the cargo van. Then she sat and waited.

The three Latinos argued back and forth. The two timid ones were more convinced to give up the chase and admit failure. The assertive one, now without a pistol or a flashlight, would not listen to them. He was convinced the only way to go was forward.

The other two were torn. They looked all around, seeing nothing in the blackness. It was like fighting a ghost, and neither believed they could win the battle.

Finally, they settled. Two of them continued the pursuit as the leader, the assertive one, yanked the Ruger from the hand of the one that wanted to return to the townhouse. The leader and the other man turned and walked down the road, away from the spot where Niki hid.

The coward retrace his steps back toward the parked vehicles. Niki predicted that he would cuddle inside the old Chevy with the doors locked. That would make it difficult for her to get to him without excess noise. She had to get to him before he reached the car.

CHAPTER TWENTY-SIX

THE RETREATING Latino had his head on a swivel, trying to search all directions at the same time. By doing so, he was seeing absolutely nothing and hearing the same. Niki crouched and followed the edge of the payment only ten steps behind the frightened man. She steadily closed the distance as they neared the iron pipe stretched across the road.

Niki waited for him to straddle the pipe, one leg touching the pavement on each side. Then her whole body flew like a smart missile, with the center of the man's brain dialed in as the coordinates.

The contact was slightly less than a ballistic missile reaching its target, but not by much to the coward. He fell stiff-legged to the other side of the pipe, his limbs extended into the air. He had no idea where he was or what happened to him.

Then Niki saw headlights approaching. She could only pray that it was not a squad car from the East Baton Rouge Parish Sheriff's Department. When she saw the outline of a great cargo van, she breathed a long sigh of relief.

"You got here right on time," she told Donna after the van parked. "I must say that you have exquisite timing."

"Great," Donna said without much enthusiasm. She was not a fan of gunfights or the darkness, especially when the two were combined.

"Come on, help me," Niki said. "I've got to get a body in the van. It'll be easier with the two of us."

"Is he dead?" Donna asked. She did not like dead bodies either.

"No, but he doesn't know that yet," Niki said.

They dragged the unconscious man to the back of the van and hoisted him in. Niki secured his hands and feet with plastic tie-wraps and put a gag in his mouth.

"Check his pockets," she instructed Donna. "Take everything you find no matter how insignificant it may seem."

"What do I do after that?" Donna asked.

"Then get back in the van behind the steering wheel and lock the door."

"And what will you be doing while I'm sitting here in the dark?"

"Waiting for the next fish to bite," Niki smiled and disappeared.

CHAPTER TWENTY-SEVEN

The other two looked frustrated. They had walked almost the entire perimeter of the sixty-two acre plot and had seen no sign of their prey. The assertive one caved.

"You go call Juan and see what he wants to do."

"What are you gonna do?" The second man asked.

"I'll keep looking. The bitch has to be here somewhere. She can't just disappear into thin air like smoke," the boss said.

The second man wasted no time expressing his opinion about the skills of Niki Dupre with his partner. He could get back to the safety of the Chevy with the third man. Inside the Chevy with a semiautomatic pistol sounded a lot better to him than traipsing through the darkness with the witch on the loose. And that is how he felt about Niki. Only a witch could fly through the air, disarming three men, then disappear.

He almost sprinted to the pipe gate. When he got there, he panted, barely able to suck in enough oxygen. Then he quit breathing altogether. Parked behind the old Chevy was a gray van. Sitting behind the steering well was the most beautiful girl she had ever seen. Under the light emitted by the streetlamp, he saw a perfectly symmetrical face, rich flowing blonde hair, and a mouth that made him drool.

The man put his Ruger away. The last thing he wanted to do was to scare the angel away. That would come later.

Donna cracked the window a tad and lifted her pert chin to talk through it. Drool fell from the Latino's mouth.

"Hey, Señorita. What you doing here?" He asked.

"My friend said they were having a party here tonight."

"Ain't nobody out here except me and my amigos," the Latino said.

"Maybe I'm early," Donna sighed. "It's all right. I can come back."

"No need to leave, Señorita. You can party with us. That way you won't be alone on a dark and scary night."

"She's not alone," Niki's voice came from behind the man.

He turned, but not fast enough. Niki's foot caught him high on his cheek, crushing the side of his orbital frame.

CHAPTER TWENTY-EIGHT

The leader, Julio, ambled down the dark streets. If only he had not lost his flashlight. If only he had not lost his gun. Then his two partners would still be with him and not back at the car telling Juan what a failure he was.

He thought about dumping the other guys, and just driving away. He was not sure where he would go. Maybe across the border to Mexico. Maybe to California. The state would protect him from the law. But it could not protect him from MS-13.

The group was huge in Southern California, due in large part to the sanctuary status it offered to illegal aliens. The policy left the citizens vulnerable to the likes of his gang, and others. He did not understand the Anglos giving up their land without a fight. In fact, their odd policies sided with people like himself over its own citizens.

No, he could not run. No matter where he went, the gang would find him sooner or later. And he knew how it meted out punishment to those who try to desert. He would rather put a bullet in his brain rather than subject himself to that kind of humiliation.

He had no choice. Julio could not find the girl without a flashlight. She could be down in a ditch a few feet from his shoes and he would not see her. He would have to go back and face Juan Valdez, no matter how painful. At least the other two men would be there to accept some of the blame unless they were plotting against him in the old Chevy.

CHAPTER TWENTY-NINE

JULIO EASED up to the old Chevy, trying to eavesdrop on his two amigos. If they were planning on turning on him, he might as well shoot them here. No sense in going back, and him taking the blame and the brunt of Valdez's ire after the leader found out they failed.

Julio slipped a leg across the pipe by and stopped. Something was not right. That is when he noticed the gray van parked behind the Explorer and the Chevy. And there was movement at its rear.

A figure stepped out in Julio's view. Instantly he knew it was not one of his amigos. Neither of them, nor any man alive, had those kinds of curves. It was also not the woman he was after. As attractive as Niki Dupre was, she was not built like this goddess.

The beautiful woman looked up and saw him. After a moment of indecision, she smiled at the Latino.

"Hey, me and your friends are about to have a party in the back of my van. They said you were too busy to join us, and we should start without you."

Julio laughed. Maybe tonight would not be a total waste. In fact, his prospects looked brighter.

"I'll party, but it'll just be you and me. Those other two, we don't need them to get in the way."

"You'll have to convince me of that," Donna said. "They're already getting undressed in the back of the van. I don't think they're gonna appreciate it if you ruin their night."

Julio strode to the back of his hand. The hourglass blonde looked even better up close. He could not find a single flaw on her entire body, though he had in mind a much more thorough and personal inspection later.

He walked past her and stuck his head inside the door.

"Hey, you assholes," he stopped when he saw his two friends stretched out on the floor with their arms and legs tied and gags in your mouths. Then his own lights went out.

CHAPTER THIRTY

Juan Valdez was furious. None of his closest allies dared come near, and his opponents found a more convenient place to be. No one wanted to get in front of the hurricane named Juan. He slapped the girl that handed him the news article so hard that she became comatose.

Most of the people in the room had read the clipping. It was another piece by the same reporter and Niki Dupre.

"The last time we talked, you said Juan Valdez, the local leader of a notorious gang, was a coward. Now you say that you have proof. What is that proof?" The reporter had asked.

"I had a brief conversation with some members of his gang. They already knew the nature of Juan Valdez. He likes to hide behind men like them and give orders from his safe refuge." Niki had replied in the article.

"Won't those men now be in hot water with the gang?"

"No," Niki had answered. "I gave them protection. If Valdez is scared of me, then he can't take retribution on his men."

"What did the men tell you about the local gang?"

"Plenty," Niki had replied. "There are forty-three members

incarcerated in the state and parish prisons awaiting trial as we speak. There are twenty-seven free members. I guess there is only twenty-four since the three that were assigned to kidnap me quit the gang."

"Did those three confirmed that Juan Valdez is the leader?"

"Absolutely," Niki replied to the reporter. "Though they say is only because he is the most brutal with those who can't defend themselves. They told me that no other man in the organization can stand him, but each of them is afraid to defy him."

"What did you find out about their operations?"

"More than enough to shut them down. I have info about their drug trafficking, sex–slave business and their protection racket. But the best information was about the money they make off of identity theft. We're taking steps to stop it now."

CHAPTER THIRTY-ONE

JUAN CALLED for a special counsel of all the top ranking members. None of them wanted to attend, but none of them dared back out on their volatile leader in his current mood.

"Has anyone heard from Julio and the other two?" He asked.

None of the six men responded. Juan slammed his fist on the table and glared at each for several seconds. None could hold his stare. They suddenly found their shoe tops interesting.

"How can one girl talk three men into deserting us?"

"Those were not our best men," one guy answered. "Julio was okay, but the other two were weaklings. They were scared."

"Scared of a woman? What have we become? Are we now scared to do battle with a female? Is that who we are?"

"The men are talking, Juan," another said. "They point out that the senorita called you a coward. Some have openly wondered if such a statement will go unpunished."

"Hell no, it won't go unpunished. I will personally skin that bitch alive. I wish they would have brought her to me."

"That's what the men are discussing," another said. "They wonder why you don't go yourself."

"Because I'm the brains behind this business. If I'm out on the streets taking care of a simple señorita, who will guide us here? No one will make the money I make?"

None of the men answered. None knew the intrinsic details of the identity theft scams and how a bunch of names and Social Security numbers could turn into a huge pile of money. Juan kept the details to himself.

"Then what do we do?" One Latino man asked.

"Who are our two best men?" Juan asked. "We will send them."

At that moment, a female computer operator stuck her head in the room. "Sorry to interrupt, but I have some bad news."

CHAPTER THIRTY-TWO

JUAN EXPLODED. He leapt across the room and slapped the woman so hard that she fell to the floor. Then he kicked her in the ribs. He was about to kick her again when two of his leaders put restraining arms around him.

"She only brought the message," one said. "Let us hear it."

Valdez stormed back to his chair. He thought about having both of his men and the woman hung upside down and skinned alive. But he was now afraid. That was the first time that any of his followers had ever restrained him. That was a bad omen.

"Get her up," he said. "Let's see what the whore has to say."

The two men helped the overweight woman to her feet and gave her a bottle of water. After a few minutes, she spoke.

"All of our computers have been taken over by a virus. It is something that says that we must pay to get our data back. Otherwise, it will erase everything."

"Don't we have backup?" He asked one of the men.

"Sure, this is no problem," the computer guru said. "I will fix everything in about five seconds."

The guru typed on his laptop. Five seconds passed without

him looking out. Fifteen seconds. Thirty seconds. After a full minute, he frowned. After three minutes, he let out a long sigh.

"Someone has infiltrated our backup servers. They have control over every bit of information we have. This is disastrous."

"Every bit of information? Even our bank accounts?" Juan asked.

At that moment, another woman peeked inside the doorway. "Senor, I hate to disturb you, but I have more bad news."

CHAPTER THIRTY-THREE

"How are our guests?" Niki asked.

She and Donna were at her fiancé's exotic game ranch about forty-five minutes north of Baton Rouge. Dalton Bridgestone, the senator, was not there at the moment, having a full slate of business in Washington D.C. He had, however, instructed his foreman, Pete, to help Niki in any way possible.

They put the three gang members in an out-barn that was built specifically to hold North American bison, more often called the American Buffalo. With steel walls two feet thick that extended from floor to the ceiling, there was little chance the men could find a way to escape.

Niki did not bother to keep the plastic ties around their wrists and ankles. She did not want them to suffer, even though they had in mind far worse things for her.

"They're grouchy," Donna replied. "I bet I've learned two dozen new Spanish curse words. Want me to teach you if you?"

"That's okay. How did the other stuff go?"

"All of their computer systems are inoperable except for their laptops. Per your instructions, they can use them to correspond to each other, but nothing else in the system will respond."

"Excellent," Niki had her friend on the shoulder. "Now, a lot of them will be sitting around with nothing to do. I wonder how long Juan will last under those conditions."

"The conditions are worse than that," Donna grinned. "While I was in their system, I accessed all their bank accounts."

"Did you find out how much money they have?" Niki asked.

"One hundred fifteen million and some change. But they had. They have it no more."

Niki raised an eyebrow.

"What did you do with it?"

"Not me?" Donna feigned innocence. "Juan made over one hundred donations to separate charities. He did it anonymously, so none of the charities will track down the source of the funds."

"I'm proud of you. What you did with the system, what you did with the money, and the information you provided about the structure of the gang. I'm sure Juan thinks his guys were the ones that ratted him out. They aren't in a pleasant position."

CHAPTER THIRTY-FOUR

Pedro and Ricky watched Niki Dupre drive the Ford Explorer into the parking lot. They were in no hurry. In their line of business, finding the target was ninety percent of the job. The rest was pure pleasure.

The two Latinos were known as the Michelangelos. Each possessed extraordinary talent wielding a sharp blade. They could take an arm off at the elbow with a single swipe. They could separate a shin from a thigh at the knee with equal ease.

Then they could peel the skin off a captive until there was nothing left but raw nerves. The victim always fainted several times during the process, but that is where they learned patience. They would wait until the poor soul woke up again before continuing. If they needed a break, they tossed alcohol onto the nerve ends. No human could withstand that pain while conscious.

After Niki exited the SUV, they saw her glanced toward the parking lot. Her gaze did not rest on the rusty pickup truck, and both were confident they had gone undetected.

When she disappeared behind her door, they got out with

the machetes at their sides. Anyone looking would have seen only a wide Latino and a small wiry one. No one would have spotted the blades of death in their hands.

When they got to the door, Ricky stepped to one side. It was the much wider Pedro's job to get them inside. And that is exactly what he did with one mighty kick.

They rushed inside, with the wide Pedro in the lead. Ricky could not see around him and bumped into the bigger man. When Pedro suddenly stopped. Ricky peeked around him and froze.

Niki Dupre was waiting for them. She held the most beautifully adorned scimitar sword either of them had ever seen.

"I figured Juan would send you two," she said. "I understand you like to play with knives. How do you like mine?"

"Very impressive, Señorita," Pedro replied. "Where did you get such a magnificent weapon? It is beyond comparison."

"This one, and two others, were built for the prophet Mohammad. I have two of them, and I'm pretty sure that the third one will be mine sooner or later. I'd bet on it."

Pedro and Ricky stared at the ornate blade, its shaft embedded with gold, silver, diamonds, and every other gem imaginable.

"It is beautiful, but it is built for show. Unfortunately, our meager machetes are built with a purpose. Why don't you give up before we have to hurt you badly?"

"Not gonna happen, boys. This little puppy was designed as the premier fighting machine in its day. I doubt if any better one has been created over the centuries. I think I'll stick with it."

"That is a shame, Señorita. There are two of us and only one of you. I'm afraid it will not be a fair fight. We would much rather take you back to Juan in one piece."

"Then I'd suggest that you quit talking and start fighting."

They did. Pedro went to his right, her left. Ricky came manner from the opposite direction. The long–legged detective backed to the edge of the hallway. At this strategic vantage point, both men converged right in front of her.

Pedro flashed his shiny blade. Niki easily parried the blow and sliced him at the bottom of the cage. Ricky tried to take advantage of her attention on Pedro and stepped from behind his wider amigo. The ornate scimitar caught him in his left shoulder, impeding any other progress.

"My goodness," Niki mocked. "Both of you boys have bobo's and you're bleeding on my carpet. Are you sure you know how to play safely with your toys?"

In response, Pedro lunged straight at the detective. The machete extended in front of like an arm. Niki slapped down on the short blade with her longer one and brought up a leg at the same time. Pedro's forearm snapped.

Ricky stood aghast at the sight. He had been in lots of fights with Pedro. The wide Latino had always held the upper hand and had always conquered the opponent. He felt as if he could not lose with Pedro as his partner. Yet–

The foot knocked out three of his teeth. He fell at the feet of his injured friend.

Donna burst through the front door, grinning. "Am I too late?"

CHAPTER THIRTY-FIVE

The article by the *Morning Advocate* went online immediately.

"Are you saying that Juan Valdez, the leader of the biggest
gang in Baton Rouge, made another attempt to kill you? Is that
true?"

"It's true," Niki replied. "But it wasn't much of an attempt.
Juan's boys are losing faith in him. They aren't confident in his
abilities."

"That's a broad statement," the reporter responded. "Can
you give me specifics?"

"Sure. The two guys that he sent over, Pedro and Ricky,
were sat down peacefully and they sought protection from me
rather than continue fighting for a madman."

"Are you saying that two killers ignored Valdez and sat
down for what could only could be called a peace conference
with you?" The reporter asked.

"There was a little tussle at first, but they saw the wisdom
in changing their commitment to the gang."

"According to the information you've already gleaned from these men that left the gang, Juan has about twenty men left. How many do you think he will send to kill you the next time?"

"Only one," Niki said. "Juan will have to come himself now. If he doesn't, then all the gang will know he is a coward."

CHAPTER THIRTY-SIX

THE FOOD at the prison was atrocious. For the inmates in isolation, like José and Rafael, whatever was on the menu was all put into a blender. It was then formed into a long roll of mush and served with water from the rusty tap.

Even as bad as it was, the roll of mush was all that the two in adjoining cells had to eat. While partitioned from the rest of the inmates population, the pair did not have commissary privileges. They could not buy chips, cookies, or tuna to supplement their meals.

José looked at his roll and grunted. "Do you want mine?"

"No, amigo. I can barely get this one down," Rafael responded.

José broke his into thirds, grabbed the closest third and tried to swallow it without chewing. The more he could avoid the acrid taste, the more he could stand it.

Rafael nibbled at his. He tried to make the consumption of the roll take as long as possible. It was a break in a long, monotonous day. They had no television, no radio, no Walkman, and no magazines. The entire boundary of entertainment for the pair of Latinos was talking to each other. Even the correctional guards that delivered the food ignored them.

Rafael was about halfway through his food roll when he first heard the gurgling sounds from the next cell. He looked over and saw José gasping and holding his throat. Foam and froth flowed from the bigger man's mouth.

Rafael looked down at the rest of his roll. He now knew the game plan to get rid of them. He stuffed the rest of the roll into his mouth. A quick death was much better than death row.

CHAPTER THIRTY-SEVEN

"How could they turn on me? On us?"

Juan Valdez walked back and forth as he ranted and raved. His inner circle was hesitant to answer the volatile leader. Among man's most inmate preferences, self-preservation tops the rest of the list. The six leaders knew the wrong response would be fatal.

The organization was in a mess. Five of the twenty-seven men had disappeared. According to the evil woman, they had switched loyalties, and now opposed the gang and Juan Valdez.

The money was gone. All the bank accounts, even those at the local banks were wiped clean. The only way to meet the payroll was to use the stash of cash Valdez kept in the fireproof safe in his office. It could not last forever.

Then Valdez made another mistake. He deposited the revenue the members earned through prostitution, drugs, and protection. He put the money in the same accounts that had been wiped out. The money stayed in those accounts for less than a minute. Then it was swept out into a big dark abyss. The gang was left without a single dollar in any account.

"Are you scared to answer me?" Valdez yelled, his face purple.

"You have a problem," one man spoke. "A lot of our members are questioning your leadership skills and your courage."

"And what do you tell them when they question you?" Valdez fumed.

"I say that our leader will do the right thing. He will stand up to Niki Dupre to prove his valor."

"Is that what all of you think? Must I again prove that I am the fiercest warrior among us?" Valdez asked.

"Yes," the man answered. "If you defeat Niki Dupre alone, then none will ever question you again. You will rule for life."

CHAPTER THIRTY-EIGHT

"At least let me put some men around you for protection," Steve Harris begged over the cell line.

"That wouldn't work," Niki responded. "I'm in East Baton Rouge Parish. Your authority stops at the parish line."

"C'mon. I know about your relationship with the chief of homicide down there. Samson Mayeaux doesn't let a little thing like geography get in his way of helping you sometimes."

"And Samson also offered to have his men protect me. I turned him down just like I'm doing with you," she said.

"And I suppose that you have a good reason," Steve said.

"If Valdez comes after me, I don't want to scare him off with a bunch of armed security guards."

"But you're setting yourself up as bait. When he strikes, it will be fast and furious. You won't have much time to react."

"It'll be okay," Niki said. "I can still smell a skunk. I'll know Valdez is here way before he gets close enough to kill me."

"I thought the same thing," Harris said. "But he got inside help to kill José and Rafael in their cells."

"How did he do it? Did he send more guys with shivs?"

"He poisoned them. Somehow he got someone inside the chow hall and put arsenic on their food rolls. We found both of them dead in their cells. Both were dead before we got there."

"They must have a lot of inside help in West Feliciana Parish, particularly with the Sheriff's Department. I don't see how you can trust anyone up there?"

"I don't," Harris responded. "I had to go back to being cynical about everyone around me. I don't trust anyone anymore, except for you."

"I appreciate that," Niki said. "Hopefully, this will be over soon."

"That's what I'm afraid, Niki. This is not a game. Valdez will play for keeps, and he is a survivor. His gut instincts have made a difference more times than we can count."

"If you're trying to make you feel better, it's not working."

"I'm trying to scare some sense into you. I've gotten kind of fond of you, and I'd hate like hell for something to happen to you."

"Me too," Niki sighed. "Me too."

CHAPTER THIRTY-NINE

OVER HALF of the bulbs were not working in the parking lot at the townhome. Niki knew this was no accident. Juan Valdez was in the parking lot somewhere. He had put out the bulbs and was ready to take advantage of his handiwork.

Niki parked in a visitor's slot instead of her usual. Might as well not make it easy for him. The long–legged detective took a quick look around the entire lot before exiting the SUV. She saw nothing.

That is, until she had taken two steps toward her town-home. Then Valdez rolled out from under a pickup truck. Niki had the S&W thirty-eight revolver aimed at his chest before he came erect. Valdez immediately threw up his hands.

"I come unarmed, Miss Dupre," he said. "I have no weapons."

"Then why are you here? All the people you sent to kill me were well armed. Why aren't you?"

"Because this has to be a fight of honor. I must defeat you with my hands to restore my honor with my people."

"So you want to fight me with your bare hands? That is something I would advise you not to do," Niki said.

"It is something I must do. I must restore the confidence of my men. I can only do that one way."

Valdez approached her, his hand still in the air. He got within a few feet and stopped.

"Please put your gun away," he said. "I swear I do not have any guns on my person. You may pat me down, if you wish."

"I would rather put my hands on a water moccasin," Niki replied. "I don't trust a word that you say."

"I am telling the truth. I know your reputation with Kempo. I'm not bad myself with martial arts. If you allow, we will see which of us learned our discipline better."

Niki still did not trust the crime boss. In her peripheral vision, she checked to see if he had brought help.

"There is no one else," he chuckled. "I assure you I am alone."

Niki replaced the thirty-eight in its holster. That's when Valdez's right hand reached to the middle of the back of his shoulders.

CHAPTER FORTY

Niki reacted in a flash. By the time Valdez pulled the Taser from its hiding place, her foot was already in motion. The squat Latino was quicker than she anticipated. He was deceptively fast, but not fast enough.

Her foot grazed his arm, causing the barbs from the first shot of the Taser to fly harmlessly overhead. But Valdez did not slow his attack. His own foot flew into Niki's lean body at the bottom of her rib cage.

The heavy blow sent the detective sprawling backward, landing on her butt. His next kick missed her jaw by an inch. She felt the breeze from the blow. An inch more accuracy would have darkened her world. She realized that Valdez was a formidable opponent.

Niki rolled away, out of range of Valdez's powerful legs. When she catapulted to her feet, he charged again. This time, Niki was prepared for his unique speed. She needed to take the advantage away from Valdez.

As the Latino flew by, the detective sidestepped and drove a foot into his right calf. She knew from experience the sharp and continuous pain this strike would cause. Before the gangster could turn around, she planted her other foot in the middle of his thigh. The combination of kicks wobbled Valdez, making the rest of his turn unsteady.

"I thought you said no weapons," Niki said. "I consider a Taser a weapon, and I consider you a man without honor."

"I needed an advantage, Señorita," he smiled. "I did not lie to you. I did not have a gun. I still do not."

"But you had a Taser. And I bet you have a knife. You would need to cut out those Taser marks. You couldn't very well drag me back to your people with those showing."

"You are as smart as they say," Valdez said, drawing a six inch steel from the small of his back.

"Please, don't insult me. A little toy like that won't do you any good. Throw it away before you get hurt."

"We will see," he said as he launched right at her. With the four inch hilt and the six inch blade, his arm extended an extra ten inches. And he was just as quick with the knife as he was with his feet.

The sharp edge caught the flap in her shirt and ripped an eight inch slice.

The guy knew how to wield the knife in his hand. Niki now knew how he rose to the leadership position for the local chapter of the gang. He was the best street fighter.

With renewed respect, Niki circled the squat man, still sporting the blade in his right hand. She kicked him in the left thigh twice with inside leg kicks and then one on the outside. She did the same to his right calf with three successive kicks.

The lunges were no longer as quick. Valdez's speed came from his powerful legs. With Niki's assault on them, they became more like soaked logs than jamming rams. The knife missed by two inches. Then four. Then six.

Niki continued the assault on his lower limbs. An outside

kick. Two inside kicks followed by another outside kick. Before long, Valdez had trouble remaining erect. He had to put his left hand on the hood of a car to remain upright.

"Give it up, Juan," Niki said. "You don't stand a chance."

The gangster pushed off the car straight at the detective. She stepped to one side. He could not get his battered legs to make a quick adjustment, and went sprawling on his face. His right hand folded underneath his body and Juan fell with the force of his whole body on his blade.

CHAPTER FORTY-ONE

Niki knew from the placement of the blade that Valdez had little time left in this world. Minutes at the most. Seconds were more probable. If she wanted any information from the crime boss, she had to get it now.

The detective turned him over to see the hilt sticking out from the lower chest. To pull it out would only speed up his death. She talked instead.

"Tell me who your contact is with the West Feliciana Parish Sheriff's Department," she said.

He cursed and tried to spit in her face. He did not have the strength to complete the latter.

"You're dying. You know that as well as I do. Who put you in this terrible position? To set you up against me?"

Niki saw the resolve in the Latino's eyes. His loyalty was his trademark. He would never betray a fellow gang member or one of their customers that hired him.

"You're not a rat. Tell me the name of the guy who cost you seven members so far and now your life. I doubt if you told anyone else, so you must tell me."

"I cannot do that," his voice barely above a whisper. "My whole life, I have never told on anyone. I won't to start now."

"If you don't tell me, what do you think they will do to those who I am protecting. They have already poisoned two of your people. José and Rafael are dead. But you know that?"

"We talked about it," he nodded. "I wanted them to escape and return to Ecuador. He wanted them dead. He said that dead men do not easily give up the secrets they know of others."

"But that's why you must tell me what you know while you're still alive."

Valdez close his eyes for a long time. At first, Niki thought the Latino had passed. Then he opened his eyes and whispered the name.

Niki sat frozen in place until Valdez died.

CHAPTER FORTY-TWO

Niki sat in the parking lot for a long time. For once, she was
uncertain if she was about to do the right thing. On this rare
occasion, she doubted her own intuition, something that rarely
failed her.

The strawberry blonde took in a deep breath and let it
escape slowly. Then she exited the Ford Explorer and strode to
the front door, showing more confidence that she felt. Her last
chance to change her mind was gone when she entered the
West Feliciana Sheriff's Department.

"Hi," the front desk officer said. "Who are you here to see
today?"

"Steve," she replied with a smile. "Is he in?"

"Sure, but he just started a meeting about the poisonings we
had. I imagine it will take a while."

"No problem. I think I have some information that will help
them come to a resolution."

Niki walked right past the front desk. When she got to the
conference room, the detective walked in without knocking.

The group was going over the roster duties from the morning of the murders. One uniform stood in front, pointing at a whiteboard full of names.

All five men turned when Niki answered.

"I'm sorry, Niki," Harris said. "This is a private meeting."

"Not anymore," the private investigator said. "I know who is responsible for those deaths. He is the contact in the Sheriff's office for the gang."

Steve Harris rose half out of his chair.

"And how would you come across this information when we can't?"

"I asked the right person," Niki replied. "Juan Valdez told me the identity right before he died."

"Valdez is dead?" Harris sank back in his chair.

"Not before he told me about you, Steve. I've got the transaction dates and the amounts where you were paid."

The Glock seventeen appeared in his hands from nowhere.

"Don't anybody move," he said, pointing the pistol all around as he rose from the chair. He backed up against the wall.

"It's over, Steve," Niki said. "There is nowhere to go."

"I can't go to jail. I killed two of the inmates. I wouldn't last through the first night."

"You should've thought of that before you got involved with the gang. What were you thinking?"

At that moment, a cop made a move at Harris. The temporary Sheriff turned and pulled the trigger. The lieutenant spun around, his blood flying in arcs.

Harris stared at the fallen officer and then stared at the pistol as though it had fired on its own. He paid no attention to Niki. A huge mistake.

She flew over the table, her external radar locked in on a

single target. When her right foot smashed into Steve's nose, the fight was over. But that did not stop private investigator. She pounded on him until the other officers pulled her away.

CHAPTER FORTY-THREE

"He sold his virtue too cheap," Niki said.

"Yep," Donna replied, after cleaning off a chicken wing. The two sat at their usual table at Linda's. "He went for thousands, not millions. You would think buying off the next sheriff of a parish would cost more."

"Especially when it comes to murdering people. Valdez paid more for a hit on the street than they paid Steve."

"Speaking of which," Donna said while reaching for a triple cheeseburger, "you knew they would put a contract out on you. They've got to get retribution for taking out their local leader and their main contact."

"I know. It never seems to end." Niki sighed. "But we'll be ready for them when they come."

NOTES

Murder of the Sheriff is the second of over twenty short mystery stories in the Niki Dupre series. It features the dynamic martial arts expert facing even greater challenges.

I have taken great literary license with the geography and data of Baton Rouge and the surrounding areas. It is a wonderful city and a great way to experience the Cajun culture. I live there for and find it to be one of the most desirable places on earth if you enjoy the outdoors, great cuisine and remarkable people.

There are so many people to thank:

My family, Linda, Josh, Dalton & Jade

David and Sara Sue

C D and Debbie Smith

My brother and sister-in-law, Bill & Pam

My sister, Debbie

My sister-in-law and her husband, Brenda & Jerry

The Sunday School class at Zoar Baptists

Jeff Trout and Chris Hall, two real men who stood beside me during my darkest hours. Jeff tried to teach me about Kempo, the ancient Chinese martial art. He soon found out I'm a slow learner.

Any and all mistakes, typos and errors are my fault and mine alone. If you would like to get in touch with me, go to my web site at
http://jimrileyweb.wix.com/jimrileybooks.

I thank you for reading **Murder of the Sheriff** and hope you will also enjoy the rest my books.

Dear reader,

We hope you enjoyed reading *Murder of the Sheriff*. Please take a moment to leave a review, even if it's a short one. Your opinion is important to us.

Discover more books by Jim Riley at
https://www.nextchapter.pub/authors/jim-riley

Want to know when one of our books is free or discounted?
Join the newsletter at
http://eepurl.com/bqqB3H

Best regards,

Jim Riley and the Next Chapter Team

Murder of the Sheriff
ISBN: 978-4-82411-775-5

Published by
Next Chapter
1-60-20 Minami-Otsuka
170-0005 Toshima-Ku, Tokyo
+818035793528

24th November 2021